I AM READING

Noisy Neighbors

NICOLA MOON

ILLUSTRATED BY
LIZ MILLION

KINGFISHER
BOSTON

For Travis—N. M.
To Nana and Grandpa Sefton with all my love—L. M.

KINGFISHER
a Houghton Mifflin Company imprint
222 Berkeley Street
Boston, Massachusetts 02116
www.houghtonmifflinbooks.com

First published by Kingfisher in 2003
This edition published in 2004
4 6 8 10 9 7 5 3
3TR/0504/AJT/FR(FR)/115MA/F

LIBRARY OF CONGRESS CATALOGING–IN–PUBLICATION DATA
has been applied for.

ISBN 0-7534-5799-7

Printed in India

Contents

Noisy Neighbors

George lived at Number Six
Acorn Road.

He loved to sit in the yard and
do the crossword puzzle in his
magazine. George dreamed that one
day he would answer all the questions
and win the big prize.

Louis lived next door to George. He loved to stand in the yard and play his trumpet. He dreamed that one day he would be a famous musician.

One day George was sitting in the yard trying to do his crossword puzzle when . . .

TRAN-TARAAH!

George was so surprised that he dropped his pen in the daffodils. "Oh, bother," he huffed.

TRAN-TRAN-TARAAH!

It was Louis, playing his trumpet.

"Excuse me, Louis," George called over
the fence. "Please could you play more
quietly? I'm trying to concentrate on my
crossword puzzle. It's very difficult today."
"Sorry," said Louis. "The trumpet isn't
a quiet sort of instrument, and I have
to practice for a very important concert.
Don't you think it's wonderful music?"

George didn't think it was at all wonderful.

"Humph!" he said and went back to his crossword puzzle.

TRAN-TRAN-TARAAH!

The music started up again, even louder than before.

"Humph! This is ridiculous!" George muttered, and he stomped indoors.

George made himself a pot of tea.

Then he opened a box of

cupcakes and settled down

in his armchair.

"At last I can concentrate!" he sighed.

The trumpet blared along
Acorn Road . . .

. . . and right into George's living room.
"Oh no!" he groaned, covering his ears
with his paws.

Now he couldn't hear the trumpet—
but he couldn't hold his pen either.

Then he noticed the tea cozy.

"Perfect!" he said, pulling it over his ears.

The tea cozy made his head hot, but

at least it muffled the noise

TRUN-TRUN-TURUUH!

But not for long . . .

TRUN–TRUN–*VROOM-VROOM-WHIRR!*

"It's getting worse!" George moaned,
pulling off the tea cozy.

"How can I think with all this noise?"
He stomped to the bathroom and found
a big bag of cotton balls.

He was just stuffing some into his ears
when . . .

BANG-BANG-BANG!

Someone was at the door.

"What is it *now*?" George wailed.

It was Louis.

"Did you hear that dreadful noise?"

he asked. "How can a musician work

with *that* going on?"

"But . . ."

said George,

pulling cotton

balls out

of his ears.

"I thought it

was you."

"*Me*? You

think *I* . . ."

VROOM-VROOM-WHIRR!

A large, shiny motorcycle came
roaring down Acorn Road.
It stopped outside Number Eight.
George and Louis stared.

Sitting on the motorcycle was their new neighbor.

"Hi! I'm Harriet," she called. "Do you like my motorcycle?"

"Humph!" said George.

"It's a little noisy. I was trying
to concentrate on a very
difficult crossword puzzle."

"And I was trying to practice
my trumpet for a very important
concert," said Louis.

"Oh dear!" said Harriet.

"Motorcycles, trumpets, and
crossword puzzles don't really mix,
do they?"

She thought for a moment.
Then she said, "Come in and have
a cup of tea. I have an idea."
"I hope it's a quick idea," mumbled
Louis. "I have a lot of practicing to do."
"I hope it's a quiet idea," muttered
George. "I have a lot of
questions to answer."

"It's a very *good* idea," said Harriet as they sat around her kitchen table. "On Mondays and Thursdays we will all

try to be quiet so that George can do his crossword puzzle."
"That *is* a good idea," said George.
"On Tuesdays and Fridays Louis can

play his trumpet as much as he likes," continued Harriet.
"That's an even better idea!" said Louis.

18

"On Wednesdays and Saturdays it will be my turn," said Harriet.

"I will be able to ride my bike and work on the engine all day long."

"What about Sundays?" asked George.

"Whose turn will it be on Sundays?"

"On Sundays," said Harriet, "we will all meet here for tea and cake."

"That's the best idea of all," said Louis, who loved to eat cake.

"The very best idea," agreed George, who loved to drink tea.

"Then it's agreed," said Harriet.

"I'll see you both tomorrow."

On the way home George stopped.

"What day is it tomorrow?" he asked.

"Sunday," said Louis.

"So . . . that means today is Saturday?"
said George.

"Oh no!" cried Louis.

"Oh . . . humph!" moaned George.

"Oh yes!" called Harriet,
putting on her helmet.
"Today is Saturday!"

VROOM-VROOM-VROOM-WHIRR!

Just in Time

George couldn't believe his eyes when
he opened his magazine one morning.
"WIN A TRIP TO MONSTER FUN PARK."
he read. "ENTER OUR CONTEST NOW!"

George had always wanted
to go to Monster Fun Park.
He was so excited that he
put three spoons of jelly into
his tea and forgot to eat his toast.

The crossword
puzzle had one
hundred questions!
George sharpened
all his pencils,
wrote a notice
that said
"DO NOT
DISTURB,"
and pinned it
to his door.
Then he settled
down to work.

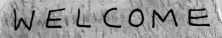

The crossword puzzle was very difficult.

George concentrated very hard.

n't hear Louis playing his trumpet

esday.

He didn't hear Harriet riding her motorcycle on Wednesday.

By Thursday only the two most difficult questions were left. George thought that Louis and Harriet would be able to help.

George went next door to see Louis.

Harriet was there, helping Louis choose

a shirt for his concert.

"Do you think I should wear the sparkly

one or the flowery one?" asked Louis.

"I like the spotty one," said Harriet.

"Yes, wear the spotty one," said George.
"Now can you help me answer *my*
questions? I could win a trip to
Monster Fun Park."
"Monster Fun Park?" said Louis.
"Wowee!"

"What are the questions?" asked Harriet.

George showed them his crossword puzzle.

"A loud musical instrument, beginning
with T?" said Louis. "It's a trumpet."
"Of course!" said George.
"Thanks, Louis."

"A noisy machine with two wheels,

beginning with M?" said Harriet.

"It must be a motorcycle!"

"That's it! Well done, Harriet,"

cried George.

George carefully wrote down the answers.
As he folded the answer sheet he noticed
the date at the top.

"Oh no!" he wailed. "We're too late!
The answers have to reach the magazine
office by twelve o'clock today.
I should have mailed this yesterday."

"We can take it ourselves," said Harriet.

"But it's miles away!" said George.

"There isn't time."

"There is if we go on my motorcycle," said Harriet. "You can both ride in the sidecar."

Louis complained about being in
the sidecar.

"My legs are squashed," he moaned.

George complained about wearing
a helmet.

"My ears are squashed," he groaned.

"Stop fussing, or we'll be late," said
Harriet. "Now, hold tight!"

They roared to

the end of Acorn Road.

"Which way now?" asked Harriet.

"Right!" said George.

"Left!" said Louis.

"Follow the signs to the town center,"
said George.

"But not so fast around the corners!"
wailed Louis, who was looking
a little green.

They raced through the intersection
and whizzed around a corner.

"Stop!" cried George as the envelope flew out of his paw and into a prickly bush.

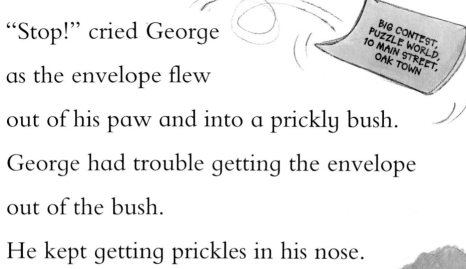

BIG CONTEST,
PUZZLE WORLD,
10 MAIN STREET,
OAK TOWN

George had trouble getting the envelope out of the bush.

He kept getting prickles in his nose.

"Hurry up!" said Harriet. "We don't have much time!"

They roared up to the magazine office.

It was two minutes until twelve.

"Are we too late?" asked George.

"Not if you run!" said Harriet.

George puffed up the stairs
and handed in his
crossword puzzle.
He was just
in time!

"Thank goodness for that!" said Louis.

"Can we go home now? *Slowly*, please!"

Soon they were sitting in Harriet's
kitchen enjoying large slices of
chocolate cake.
Louis, who was feeling better,
had two pieces.

"When will you know if you've won?"
asked Harriet.
"Not until next week," George sighed.

The next few days seemed very long. Louis couldn't concentrate on playing his trumpet.

Harriet couldn't concentrate on fixing her motorcycle.

George couldn't concentrate on anything at all. He thought he would burst if he kept waiting.

Then at last one morning a fat, gold envelope dropped onto the doormat. His paws were shaking as he tore it open and read:

"CONGRATULATIONS!
YOU HAVE WON FIRST PRIZE."

George rushed outside.

Louis was there, helping Harriet polish her motorcycle.

"Harriet! Louis! I've won! I'm going to Monster Fun Park!" he shouted.

"Well done, George!" said Louis and Harriet. "We knew you could do it."

"You both helped me win," said George, "and you're coming with me—I've got three tickets!"

They had a wonderful day at
Monster Fun Park.
"Hold tight!" said Harriet
as they went on the roller
coaster for one last ride.

"This time I'm going to keep my eyes open!" said Louis.

"So am I," said George.

"Here we go!"

WHEEEEE!

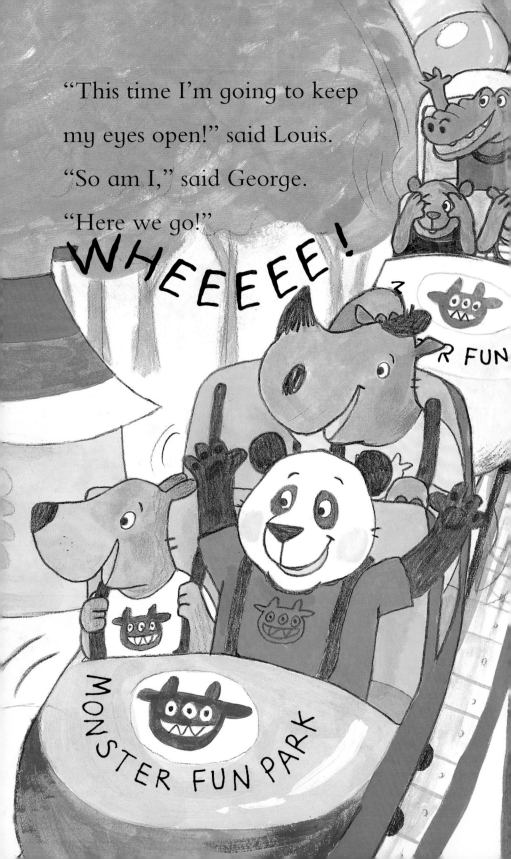

About the author and illustrator

Nicola Moon used to be a science teacher, but now she writes books full time. She says, "I feel sorry for George with those noisy neighbors. But they are such special friends, I don't think he would ever change them. Do you?"

Liz Million loves illustrating children's books, and she regularly visits schools and libraries to talk about her work. She says, "George reminds me of my grandpa. He enjoys doing crossword competitions. Sometimes he wakes my nana up at night when he's trying to think of the answer to a difficult question. Poor Nana!"

Strategies for Independent Readers

Predict
Think about the cover, illustrations, and the title of the book. What do you think this book will be about? While you are reading think about what may happen next and why.

Monitor
As you read ask yourself if what you're reading makes sense. If it doesn't, reread, look at the illustrations, or read ahead.

Question
Ask yourself questions about important ideas in the story such as what the characters might do or what you might learn.

Phonics
If there is a word that you do not know, look carefully at the letters, sounds, and word parts that you do know. Blend the sounds to read the word. Ask yourself if this is a word you know. Does it make sense in the sentence?

Summarize
Think about the characters, the setting where the story takes place, and the problem the characters faced in the story. Tell the important ideas in the beginning, middle, and end of the story.

Evaluate
Ask yourself questions like: Did you like the story? Why or why not? How did the author make the story come alive? How did the author make the story fun to read? How well did you understand the story? Maybe you can understand it better if you read it again!